VANISHING POINT

POINT

Titles in Teen Reads:

Badger Publishing Limited, Oldmedow Road, Hardwick Industrial Estate, King's Lynn PE30 4JJ
Telephone: 01438 791037

www.badgerlearning.co.uk

VANISHING POINT

CHERYL LANYON

Vanishing Point ISBN 978-1-78464-611-0

Publisher: Susan Ross
Senior Editor: Danny Pearson
Editorial Coordinator: Claire Morgan
Copyeditor: Cambridge Publishing Management
Designer: Bigtop Design Ltd
Cover: © Peter Carroll / Alamy Stock Photo

2 4 6 8 10 9 7 5 3 1

CHAPTER 1

A NEW-LOOK ELLA

Ella's Diary — 19 January

Wow! First day back at school since I was ill and it was amazing. Even the teachers were nice to me! For once, everyone was paying attention to me and asking questions and saying nice things. Can you imagine? Fat, boring me as the star of the show! Well, of course they all noticed I'd lost a load of weight and said I was looking good.

Even Jaz and Lucy, the 'Cool Girls', said I looked fantastic. They chatted with me at lunch and said we should hang out together on Friday after school. They've never even spoken to me in the past. It was a nice feeling, like I was popular. They said they liked my short haircut, which I only had because my hair got so hot and sweaty when I was lying in bed feeling awful. I've never dared get my hair cut into a proper style before — I thought people would laugh at me because it wasn't cool or something. I even caught Craig taking a sneaky look at me — yeah, Craig, only the fittest guy in the year! I don't think he's ever noticed I exist before. It was really fun and made me feel like a 'new me'.

So I'm going to write this diary about my new life and adventures as the slim and lovely Ella! I'm writing in this book so I can put down everything I think and not worry that someone's going to hack my computer and find it. I can stick in pictures and tickets and other things too.

Life's not all brilliant, though. I've missed a load of lessons and it's going to be a nightmare catching up. I'll just have to work extra hard because I don't want to get left behind. And I don't want my grades going down — not after I've worked so hard.

I'm pretty hacked off at home too. It's five months since Dad left and I've only had one phone call and a couple of texts from him — even while I was ill. And he never answers my calls. I suppose he's too busy with his new woman to think about his wife and pudgy kid living the same old dull life here. Doesn't he miss us at all? How could he just go away and forget about me? Mum mopes around all the time and cries when she thinks I don't notice. I wish I could talk to Dad. It feels like my whole family's fallen apart and there's nothing I can do.

When Ella came back to school after six weeks off with glandular fever, everyone noticed the change. She'd always been one of those quiet girls nobody noticed. She did well in all the school subjects, but didn't really belong to any group or have any best friends. She didn't seem to care much about how she looked and was, well, to put it bluntly, a bit on the heavy side. But that day she came back, it was like she'd had a makeover. She was much slimmer and had cut her rather straggly chestnut hair into a shiny bob. She smiled a lot as the other kids crowded around and paid her compliments. Nobody had seen her smile much before — it lit up her face.

Jaz and Lucy, one dark and curvy, the other blonde and willowy, noticed her for the first time.

They admired her new look and drew her into their gossipy gang. Ella laughed with them, her eyes shone with surprise and pleasure, and she felt a million dollars.

Craig was tall and good-looking, with smooth, dark skin and large, brown, almond-shaped eyes. He was a popular guy. He joked a lot with his mates and was friendly to everyone, but he didn't pick out any girls for special attention (although many of them would have been happy if he had). But that day he noticed Ella. Of course he saw how attractive she looked, but what really caught his eye was how she blossomed with all the attention. Her laugh, which he'd never heard before, was light and sexy.

Ella's Diary — 30 January

I can't believe it! Everything's soooooooo cool!

Getting to know Jaz and Lucy better. Surprised to find they're actually quite into reading, like me. They're not really bothered about curriculum books, which is why they don't do so well in English at school. Jaz is into thrillers, like some of those Swedish ones they've made into TV series and films. Lucy prefers sci-fi and fantasy and some of that sounds quite fun too. It's strange, just because they were so cool and gorgeous, I thought they were airheads. But they're not, and we have really good talks about everything — and what they know about beauty products is pretty wild!

I'm going to get a Saturday job in a shop in town to save some money for new clothes. Well, most of my old clothes are way too big now. Anyway, I can wear things I never dared to before! I'm going to need to keep slim. But that's not too hard. I'll become vegetarian and just eat loads of healthy stuff like salad and fruit.

Just to inspire me, I've cut some pictures of models I like out of the Sunday magazines and stuck them in this diary. They look so amazing — how do they do it? I'll never look like them, but they make me want to keep trying!

CHAPTER 2

GETTING IN SHAPE

"What have you got for lunch, Ella?" asked Jaz peering over into Ella's plastic box.

"Salad," replied Ella, filling her fork with leaves.

"What kind?"

"It's just mixed leaves, cucumber, celery, and some cottage cheese."

"Really? Is that all? *That* can't fill you up," said Jaz as she tucked into her tuna-mayo sandwich and grabbed a handful of sweet chilli crisps from the bag. "How do you keep going on that?"

"It's fine," said Ella. "It makes me feel kind of pure and healthy. I couldn't eat all those carbs — I'd swell up like a balloon," she added, wrinkling her nose at Jaz's lunchtime choices. "And mayo's got far too many calories for me. Salad doesn't feel heavy on your stomach and I've got plenty of energy, so it's no problem."

"You should come to the gym with us," said Lucy. "Use up some of that energy if you've got so much."

"I think I might," Ella replied. "I can probably afford the membership now I've got a Saturday job."

Jaz and Lucy went to the gym twice a week, Tuesdays and Fridays. Ella began to go with them. A personal trainer asked her what her aims were and she told him she felt she still had some flab to lose and wanted to look more toned. He showed her how to do a good all-round routine on the machines. Ella took to it straightaway and soon she started to love the way it made her feel.

If she'd eaten a bit more than she'd meant to (Jaz always had chocolate and Ella couldn't always resist), she could push herself a bit harder and longer on the machines. Then she felt that she'd 'paid' for her moment of weakness.

"Come on, Lucy," urged Ella, sitting next to Lucy on the shoulder press machines, "you can do more than that. I'm aiming for ten sets."

"Slow down, girl," moaned Lucy, "I'm done!" She dropped her arms, breathing heavily.

But Ella loved the high she got from pushing herself. She could feel the calories burning as she pounded the treadmill, setting it faster and steeper than her friends; or as she rowed like she was in an Olympic event. She was pleased with the effect of the exercise on her arms and legs, stomach and bottom.

Ella's Diary — 15 February

I got a job in Loulou's on the High Street. It's minimum wage, of course, but it soon adds up — and I get a discount too. There's a black body-con dress I'm saving up for, but I've still got some fat to lose before I can wear it. I saw this fabulous red-headed model wearing something similar (though probably ten times more expensive) in the newspaper. She looked amazing. The dress was skin-tight (without a bulge in sight!) and she had these fab slim, toned arms and legs. It's going in the diary, of course!

Now I've got a job, I don't get so much time at weekends for schoolwork. Mum's still in a bad mood about Dad and she keeps on at me, asking if I've caught up with everything yet. I know she's expecting me to get good GCSEs next year so I mustn't get behind. I'm trying my best. I've made a timetable for catching up and I'm making progress. I do sometimes have to carry on until eleven or midnight on a Sunday to finish my regular homework and the extra. I'm still scared I'm not doing enough.

CHAPTER 3

HE CAN'T MEAN ME!

In the changing room after a gym session during half term, Jaz said, "Are you lot coming for a juice in the gym café? Some of the guys from school are playing five-a-side here tonight and I said we might see them in there afterwards."

"Well, I certainly need a drink," said Lucy.

"Me too," agreed Ella.

In the café they found Stefan, Ali, Craig and Joe downing pint glasses of water. They were freshly showered, but still had colour in their faces from their game.

"Hi, guys," said Stefan with a wave. "Come and join us. Can we treat you to some best-quality tap water?"

"Whoo, big spender!" teased Jaz.

The girls joined them at the table. Craig said, "Sit down," nodding at the chair next to him.

With a shock, Ella realised he was looking at her. *He can't mean me!* she thought. But Craig reached out and grabbed her sports bag and pulled her gently towards him. She sat down next to him with a bump.

"So, you're looking fit," he said. "Fit and *healthy* I mean, of course." His eyes twinkled cheekily. "What have you been up to?"

Ella could feel her cheeks flush. "Oh, you know, just the usual workout."

"Well, lookin' good," he said, nodding with approval.

"Who's going to Ted's party on Saturday?" asked Ali to the whole group. To Ella's relief, Craig turned his attention to them and started joking about whether Ted would finally pluck up the courage to ask Kamini to his party. Everyone knew he'd fancied her for ages.

Later that week, Ella's mobile pinged and there was a message from Craig! Her heart began thumping as she read it.

Ella's Diary — 19 February

OMG, I can't believe this is happening! Calm down, girl, start at the beginning!

So, I joined the gym that Jaz and Lucy go to and started using the machines. I caught on pretty quickly and after a few sessions I was as good as them — better, in fact, if I say so myself. I can make myself go on while the other two collapse puffing. I seem to be losing weight as well as getting toned, which is fine. I really, really don't want to go back to the size I was before.

Well, one night last week, we met Craig and some other guys from school at the gym and Craig made me sit by him and told me I was looking good. Typical me, I blushed and couldn't think of anything to say, but I couldn't help being pleased. Then, on Wednesday, he texted me and asked me out! I was gobsmacked! He asked me to the movies on Friday.

When I told Jaz and Lucy they were dead impressed. They said they were jealous, but then they were really nice about it. I said I wasn't sure I was ready for this, but they just told me not to be stupid.

So I accepted, but I honestly don't know if it's a good idea. What will we talk about all evening? And I don't fancy having to meet up with a crowd of his friends. I can't believe he really likes me. And what can I wear that won't make me look fat? It's a bit of a nightmare, really. Perhaps I should make an excuse and say I can't go?

CHAPTER 4

THE FIRST DATE

Ella did go in the end. She met Craig in the mall. He wanted to treat Ella to pizza before the film, but Ella said she had already eaten. She hadn't, but there was no way she was eating a calorie-crammed pizza. She sat and drank a glass of water while Craig ate his Four Seasons. He felt a bit strange, eating while Ella watched, but she insisted that he should go ahead.

Craig was easy company and Ella found she could talk to him no problem. She found out that Craig wanted to be an IT engineer and had great plans for a brilliant career. Maybe he'd even go to Silicon Valley in California if he could get a job there. His dad had left the family, so he and Ella had that in common. Craig was the oldest of three brothers so he felt he should look after the family. He didn't want his brothers getting into trouble with gangs or drugs or other bad stuff. He loved talking about the music he was into and wanted to be a DJ as well as an IT genius. Ella told him about her plans to get good GCSEs and then go on to A levels and maybe college, if she could. They were almost late for the movie.

They enjoyed the film, but Ella said she had to get home when he wanted to meet up with friends later. She was worrying about how she'd missed her usual gym session and decided she'd better do a workout in her room when she got home.

Ella's Diary — 20 March

I'm really glad I'm writing this diary in a book I can hide. I wouldn't want anyone reading it. They'd think I'm crazy. Why? I think about food all the time. But I can't eat more than I'm 'allowed', even if I'm starving —

which I am, quite often. I can't even look at some foods. I'm afraid they'll make me fat. Instantly. How mad is that? I know how many calories are in everything and I count them endlessly.

And there's something else — no, I can't write it. But I'm going to — I've got to say it to someone. So, it's like there's this voice talking to me all the time when I think about food or eating. I mean, it's not a real person or anything, it's just there, *in my head. It tells me I'll feel better if I only eat half of my apple; or life will be good if only I can lose a few more pounds, things like that. God, people would think I'm nuts if I told them about this — maybe I am?*

By the way, I've decided not to see Craig any more. Jaz and Lucy think I've lost it, but I just can't do it right now. We've been out a couple more times, and he's nice, but I can't cope with a relationship at the moment. Anyway, he nearly always wants to eat or drink something. I can't stand all this fast food and fizzy drinks. It's like putting poison in your body and I only want to eat and drink pure, clean things.

And I don't have time, either. In spite of all my studying, I'm still sure I've missed something or not learned it well enough. I'm really worried about the exams coming up this year. I hope I don't do really badly.

CHAPTER 5

JAZ AND LUCY GET WORRIED

At parents' evening, Ella's teachers told her mum that Ella was doing well, particularly as she'd missed so much at the start of the year. When Ella's mum told her what the teachers had said, Ella couldn't really believe it. She felt she had to push herself even harder.

She began to spend her lunchtimes alone in the library, saying she needed to put in the extra hours. It also meant that no one could watch her eating. Jaz and Lucy had started to make comments about how thin she was. She didn't need their opinions. She thought to herself, *I'm in control now. Nobody can tell me what's right for my body.*

As she opened her books to start working, she took out her lunch: two rice crackers with a smear of Marmite and three slices of cucumber each. She ate these slowly, chewing each bite 100 times before swallowing. When they were gone, she took her apple and cut it carefully into quarters with a knife. She cut out the core, then examined the four wedges carefully. She picked the two she thought were slightly bigger and threw them in the wastepaper bin, then ate the two smaller ones.

Jaz and Lucy were leaning against a wall chatting as usual.

"Don't you think Ella might be overdoing this health kick?" said Jaz. "I mean, she's looking really skinny. You can see it in her face — her cheeks are hollow; and her collar-bones stick out like knobs. It's not actually that attractive. And she hardly hangs out with us anymore."

"I know what you mean," said Lucy. "She's acting quite strange. I wonder if anything's wrong at home, maybe."

"Yeah. And it's funny. Sally said she saw Ella at the gym on Wednesday. Well, she comes with us on Tuesdays and Fridays, and she said she was thinking of going on Sundays as well. And you know how hard she pushes herself when she's there. If she's doing that more or less every day, it's no wonder she's losing weight."

"Do you reckon we should say something to her?"

"No — I dunno — well, what could we say? You know how she always says she's never going to get fat again. She won't want to hear that we think she's gone too far."

Ella's Diary — 20 April

Oh, God! Why's everyone being such a pain? Mum's still the same as ever, but now she's after me about being thin as well. She hasn't noticed up to now. She's always still at the office when I get home, so I can eat what I want and she doesn't know how much I have — as long as there's a dirty plate in the dishwasher. And I'm always cold anyway, so I wear big, baggy sweaters so she can't see anything. I knew she'd try to make me eat if she noticed my weight.

So that's Mum, Jaz and Lucy all getting at me. What's with all of them? Can't they see the lumps and bumps and flab I still need to get rid of?

Anyway, me and Mum had a row. I told her I was fine. I yelled at her, actually. I'm in my room now, keeping out of the firing line.

CHAPTER 6

ESCAPE TO BRIGHTON

Jaz and Lucy had been planning a few days in Brighton during May half term for ages. Jaz's older sister was at college there and said they could use her flatmate's room as she was going away. They had invited Ella back in February and she'd been pleased. It proved that Jaz and Lucy were really her friends and Ella had felt excited.

"Cool," she had said. "The seaside!"

"And there's lots of great boutiques in The Lanes," Lucy had said. She'd been to Brighton once before with Jaz.

"And there's plenty of guys from the Uni," Jaz had added. "If it's warm, they'll all be on the beach and we can check them out!"

"You airhead!" had joked Lucy. "I thought you liked Uni boys for their brains!"

But now it was nearly time to go to Brighton, Ella had changed her mind. How would she be able to eat as she liked and exercise every day with her friends there? They were bound to comment and make a fuss. But she knew if she couldn't stick to her routine she would feel like a bad person and be miserable. She couldn't cope with being with Jaz and Lucy all day and night for several days. She just wanted to be on her own. But they had bought the train tickets months ago to make sure they got the cheapest fare. Ella tried telling Jaz and Lucy she didn't want to go, but they wouldn't listen.

***

They arrived at Brighton station and followed Jaz's sister's directions to her flat, which wasn't far. Jaz and Lucy had giggled and taken selfies on the train. Ella smiled but didn't say much.

Jaz's sister's flat was on the third floor of a tall building a few streets back from the sea. Seagulls cried around the windows and they could just see the sea if they stood on tiptoe and looked out of the bathroom window. Jaz's sister said "Hi" and showed them her flatmate's room. Then she went out to meet her friends. The flatmate's room was quite small, but had a double bed two of them could share and enough room for the third girl to sleep on cushions on the floor.

"Let's go and explore!" cried Jaz and they went out into the sunshine.

They found the beach and walked along the pebbles, enjoying the sound of the sea and looking at the groups of people sitting or playing with kites and balls. Ella was determined to act normal and tried to join in with Jaz and Lucy's cheerful banter and happy laughter.

At last, Lucy said, "I'm starving! Let's get something to eat."

"Yeah, what shall we have?" joined in Jaz enthusiastically.

"Um, sure," said Ella. "I'm just feeling a bit chilly. I think I'll go back to the flat and get my hoodie. You find somewhere nice and you can text me how to get there. I'll join you later. Anyway, I'm not really hungry."

"Oh, *Ella*," sighed Jaz. "Come on, we're on holiday, for God's sake! No diets now!"

"But you must be hungry!" said Lucy. "We haven't had anything since on the train."

"No, not really," said Ella moodily, looking at the ground.

"Is anything wrong?" asked Lucy, more kindly.

"No! Why should there be anything wrong?" snapped Ella. "I'm not hungry, OK? I'll catch you later."

Then she turned and strode off quickly, back along the beach towards the flat.

"Ella!" shouted Jaz after her.

But Ella kept on walking.

"What the…?" said Jaz. "What did I say?"

"I don't know. She's in one of her strange moods. Maybe we can talk to her later," said Lucy.

Ella's Diary — 2 June

At the flat in Brighton. I'm so sick of being hassled. I didn't want to come on this stupid trip and now I know it was a big mistake. People just can't leave me alone to be me. I'm not like them. If I start eating just anything, I know I'll never stop. I'll eat and eat and swell and swell until I'm a huge, shapeless blob. That mustn't happen!

I can't stand this. I'm going out for a run. I've got to get some exercise or I'll go crazy.

* * *

Jaz and Lucy found a chip shop and ate some delicious fish and chips. When they got back to the flat, Ella wasn't there.

"Where is she? Oh no! You don't think she's gone home, do you?" asked Lucy anxiously.

"No, her overnight bag's still here," replied Jaz. She lifted the bag up by one strap to show Lucy and a book fell out. It dropped to the floor and fell open.

"Oops," said Jaz as she bent to pick it up. Then, "What's this?"

She had the book in her hand and was looking at a page of Ella's writing.

"If I start eating just anything, I know I'll never stop..."' read Jaz. "I think it's a diary," she added. She flipped back a few pages. *"'I can't eat more than I'm 'allowed', even if I'm starving — which I am, quite often.'"* Jaz flicked through some more pages, reading out parts of Ella's diary.

Jaz stopped and looked up at Lucy. Lucy had her hand over her mouth, her eyes wide in shock.

"That's awful," whispered Lucy. "She's really sick. What do we do?"

"I don't know. I feel terrible," said Jaz. "I thought she was just overdoing the dieting thing a bit, but it looks like she's got a serious eating problem. We've got to help somehow. We'd better try to talk to her."

"But she'll go ballistic if she finds out we've read her diary."

"I know. We're going to have to think about this."

Ella's Diary — 9 June

I haven't really seen Jaz and Lucy since Brighton. It's probably for the best. I don't need the bother.

Me and Mum haven't spoken much since our row, but she tried to have a 'serious talk' with me last weekend. God, it was embarrassing! She came over all 'understanding' and 'sympathetic' and wanted to know if I was worried about something.

Then she asked if I was ill. Wanted to know why I was off my food and blah, blah, blah... She actually said she'd noticed I hadn't put tampons on the shopping list recently, and was everything OK 'in that department'? Was there something I wanted to tell her? Did I think I should see a doctor? I wanted to curl up and die! I told her everything was OK and I was just stressed out by exams, like everyone else. I said it would be fine once the exams were over and promised to go out for a meal with her at the end of term to get her off my back. (Just kidding, right? There's no way. I'll get out of it somehow!)

Nobody understands. I'm different. I can beat my hunger. I've got rules and I stick by them. That's strong! Anyway, if I don't stick by them, I've failed. And that weird voice keeps reminding me that I'm still fat and disgusting, I should hate myself for being such a lump of lard.

And exams start next week. Help!

CHAPTER 7

SEARCHING FOR ANSWERS

Jaz and Lucy were seriously worried about Ella, but they didn't know what to do. They got together one afternoon after school, determined to talk it over.

"We've got to do something, Jaz. We've got to help Ella somehow," said Lucy in a troubled voice.

"I know. I feel the same," said Jaz. Then, in a firm voice, "Right, we need some advice. Let's look it up."

She took out her tablet and tapped in 'eating disorders' and lots of websites came up. She opened one that looked official and read out,

"'Eating disorders are serious mental illnesses. They include anorexia, bulimia and binge eating…'"

"Yeah, I wondered about anorexia," said Lucy. "Let's see what it says about that."

Jaz tapped on the link. She read out phrases as they both read the information, "'mostly girls, but boys as well… keep their body weight low by dieting and excessive exercise… distorted image of their body… think they're fat… hide their behaviour…'"

"My God, that's Ella exactly, isn't it? Especially when you think of those things we read in her diary," said Lucy. "We should have realised before. I wonder what we should do?"

"In this 'How you can help' section it says the most important thing is for the anorexic person to get professional help. But to do that, they have to admit they have a problem and be willing to get help," said Jaz. "All friends can do is be supportive and encourage them to do that."

"I don't think Ella will listen to us," said Lucy. "She just gets angry if we mention her weight."

"I know," said Jaz. "I think we need to get some adult involved, like someone Ella respects. I don't know her mum, do you? Who else could we ask?"

Lucy thought for a moment. "What about Miss Martin? Ella really likes her, and she was great when we got worried about Janine after her dad died," she said.

"Good idea. We'll do it tomorrow."

Both girls felt a bit relieved. They'd thought of a way to do something, at least. Maybe Miss Martin would know what to do next.

Ella's Diary — 15 June

I can't eat anything without feeling so guilty. So then I have to eat less and fit in extra exercise as punishment. I daren't go to the gym any more often — Mum would freak — so I do loads of workouts in my room. And then I have

less time to do my revision, so then I go to bed really late, and then I'm exhausted… English exam tomorrow —
I know I'm going to fail!

CHAPTER 8

ACTION!

The next day, Jaz and Ella spoke to Miss Martin. The teacher listened carefully to what they had to say. She was shocked when they told her what they'd read in Ella's diary.

"I've noticed that Ella's behaviour has changed," she said. "She seems very withdrawn. And, now you mention it, she has got even thinner since she lost weight at the beginning of the year. But I didn't realise it was anything this serious."

She told the friends that they had done the right thing to come to her and that she would talk to the School Counsellor. Jaz and Lucy were glad someone was going to help, but begged Miss Martin not to say anything to Ella or anyone else about reading Ella's diary — Ella would hate them for that. She said she'd have to mention it to the Counsellor, but it wouldn't be passed on to anyone else.

* * *

Miss Martin and the School Counsellor talked to Ella together. Ella put on her best 'cheerful and normal' act and stubbornly insisted she was perfectly OK. The Counsellor didn't push her, but said she'd like to talk to Ella once a week for a while. Ella rolled her eyes and sighed, "Fine! Can I go now?"

The Counsellor also got in contact with Ella's mum. In a way, her mum was relieved to hear that others had noticed Ella's behaviour. She had been worried but hadn't been able to watch Ella closely since she was out all day. She told the Counsellor she'd tried to talk to Ella about whether she was eating enough or if she was feeling unwell, but that Ella just blew up angrily.

The school advised Ella's mum to try to get Ella to see a doctor, as a first step to getting proper help. So she tried, but Ella refused, and she didn't want to force her. Her mum felt desperate. What had she done to make Ella so unhappy she starved herself?

***

One day, while Ella was exercising in her room, her phone pinged. She ignored it and carried on with her routine. But once she'd finished, she picked up her mobile and gasped. There, on the screen, it said 'Dad'. She clicked on the message immediately and read, "Coming to see you sweetheart. Saturday at 10.00am. Love you, Dad x".

She didn't know what to feel. Excited, of course. Pleased, happy — she'd actually be seeing him in two days' time. And on his own, it sounded like. No girlfriend in tow. But then she felt scared. Suspicious, annoyed. Angry even. Why was he coming now? Had Mum said something to him? Was he going to lecture her, like everyone else?

Ella's Diary — 18 June

Saw Dad today. Mum said she was going out so I could talk to him on my own, which I suppose was nice of her. He rang the doorbell and I let him in which seemed weird, as if he was a stranger. I felt shy, but he just said, "Darling!" and hugged me. I was so happy to see him. We talked and talked. It was great. We talked about school, and exams, and my Saturday job, and which TV series I was following. It was just like the old days.

Then, of course, he had to go and spoil it. He said Mum had told him she was worried about me and asked me what was going on. So, he's just like all the rest after all! I hoped he might see how hard I've been trying and how much I've changed from the chubby little kid I was, and say he was coming home… but no such luck!

He went on about how I didn't look well and Mum was upset and he'd heard the school had got involved — all that crap. But it was quite nice when he said he was worried about me too, and didn't want to see his daughter like this, but just wanted me to get some help. I told him I wasn't sick, but he said it wasn't natural to starve myself and that I needed to see someone. I can't believe I actually agreed to see a doctor — only because he said it was making him so unhappy to see me like this.

Well, if it makes him feel better, I guess I can talk to a doctor once. They can't make me do anything I don't want to. And perhaps Mum will leave me alone too.

CHAPTER 9

VANISHING POINT

Jaz and Lucy still thought about Ella a lot. Although it was difficult to understand, they were trying to accept that Ella's anorexia was a mental illness. Trying to be logical with her wouldn't work. Ella was in the grip of the anorexia and the anorexia was telling her what to do. Only Ella herself could decide she didn't want to be ill any more. But they were determined to let Ella know that they cared and were still her friends.

One Friday after exams were over, they managed to persuade Ella to come to Lucy's house with them after school. Ella made excuses, but they pleaded with her. They said they wanted ideas for

Lucy's birthday party which was coming up in a few weeks' time. They made it clear they needed Ella to help with ideas for a fancy-dress theme, and the music. They knew she wouldn't want to talk about the food or drinks.

They settled in Lucy's bedroom and swapped ideas for the party. Ella got quite lively and came up with an 'aliens' theme to appeal to Lucy's love of science fiction. After all, aliens were all shapes and sizes. They could be beautiful space maidens with silver hair and green lips if they wanted. And Ella had always enjoyed talking about music, and joined in almost like she used to.

They all laughed when they remembered Stefan's impression of 'dad dancing' at a party, and Lucy said, "It's great to see you laughing, Ella. It's cool when we can have a laugh together, like before. Sometimes these days it's like our old friend has gone and an alien has taken her place."

"What do you mean?" said Ella defensively.

"It's kind of sad, like we've lost our friend," said Jaz. "You don't seem happy, Ella. And we hate seeing you not taking care of yourself. You know, if we can help, you can talk to us any time. Or if you can't talk to us, it might not be such a bad idea to go and see a therapist or something."

Ella went tense and wouldn't look at them, "I'm fine," she said and sank into silence.

She left soon afterwards.

Ella's Diary — 23 June

Come on, anorexia, you've got to help me. You're my only true friend — you know what I need. We can't let other people try to make me fat, can we? Jaz and Lucy mean well, but they don't know how I feel.

The voice is getting louder and stronger in my head. I'm afraid to look at food because the voice will say, "Don't touch that! You're greedy and disgusting." And on and on…

Sometimes I dream of a vanishing point in the far distance, where I'm light and weightless like a wisp of mist. If only I could get there…

CHAPTER 10

HOPE ON THE HORIZON

Ella couldn't escape from anorexia. She went to see a doctor, but just lied to him about her dieting and exercise and he seemed to think her weight loss was not unusual after the glandular fever. No matter how concerned her parents, friends and school became, she refused to accept that anything was wrong. Her family did all they could. Her mum found a support group that helped her find ways to cope with Ella's anorexia better. She asked Ella's dad to get involved and he started to visit Ella more often. He told her he loved her and wanted her to get well.

At first, it all had the opposite effect. Ella liked the attention. She was seeing more of her dad. Anorexia had done this! She wasn't stopping now.

But slowly, slowly, she began to feel bad for making her family and friends so unhappy. She also grew tired of fighting the noisy, bullying voice that echoed more and more in her head. Months later, she woke up one day and thought, *I don't want to do this anymore.* She didn't know where this surprise thought had come from, but it shone strongly in her mind.

She told her mum she was ready to get some help. It took a while, but at last they found a fairly local eating disorders clinic where they could see her. Ella found it hard to trust the experts there at first. But the therapist didn't try to make her eat. They talked about the things Ella got from anorexia — attention, control, feeling special and different. And they also talked about the things anorexia would take away from her if she carried on. She could become seriously ill, and then A Levels, college and a normal life would be impossible. A nutritionist planned a diet with her, so she could put on weight bit by bit until she reached a healthy target.

It would take a long time and she would need lots of support from the clinic experts and her family and friends. Sometimes she slipped back into her anorexic habits. She still couldn't bear the thought of being fat. But now she could see that the horizon held hope, not just a vanishing point.

Ella's Diary

Oh, God! It's so hard sometimes. I say to myself again and again, like a chant: A Levels, college, job; A Levels, college, job; A Levels, college, job. What I really mean is life! I want my life. Not the anorexic life, but the life I'm supposed to have.

* * *

Five years later

Ella turned to the left, then to the right, frowning as she looked at herself in the mirror. Was that a bit of a bulge above the waistline of her jeans? She shook her head. "*No*, don't think like that," she told herself, sternly. "I don't have to think like that anymore."

Ella was getting ready to go out with Michael. He was on the same course at college and they'd been made partners on a project. Ella liked how they had different ways of looking at things. It made the project more interesting. She also came to like his silly jokes, and his floppy dark hair, and the way he looked at her... Without realising it, she found she really looked forward to their time together.

One week he was ill. Ella was restless and couldn't get on with the project. Suddenly she found she was thinking, "I *wish* Michael was here!" The longing she felt surprised her.

And now Michael had asked her out and she was happy. It was going to be a success, she'd make sure of that. She could hardly believe it was happening: A Levels, college, and now Michael. The chant that had helped her begin her journey away from anorexia was coming true — and she hadn't even dared add 'boyfriend' to her list of dreams.

She'd have to tell him about the anorexia, but not tonight. Tonight she was just going to be Ella.

THE END

Help and Advice

If you think someone you know has an eating disorder, or you think you may have one yourself, there's a lot of information you can find on the internet. Some useful sites are listed below. Always try to make sure you are looking at a site that is about explaining what eating disorders are and what help is available, not sites that encourage unhealthy eating habits. But looking at the internet alone is not enough. Remember that the most important thing is to seek professional help.

National Health Service (NHS)
www.nhs.uk/conditions/Eating-disorders

Beat
https://www.b-eat.co.uk

National Centre for Eating Disorder (NCED)
http://eating-disorders.co.uk

Mind
www.mind.org.uk

ABOUT THE AUTHOR

Cheryl is a writer and editor who loves words (and sentences and paragraphs… you get the picture) and reads — a lot! She devours novels and has a particular fondness for science fiction (not the battles-with-aliens sort but the what-life-might-be-like-in-the-future ones). She has written non-fiction and therefore knows lots of useless facts. It makes her handy on quiz nights.

She lives in London, where she grows flowers and vegetables; goes to the theatre and cinema loads; and likes walking along the River Thames.